Pippin and Mabel

Pippin and the Bones

For Chris — K.V.J.

For Simon, Emma, Ali and Charlie — B.L.

Text © 2000 K.V. Johansen
Illustrations © 2000 Bernice Lum

Kids Can Press acknowledges the financial support of the Ontario Arts Council, the Canada Council for the Arts and the Government of Canada, through the BPIDP, for our publishing activity.

Published in Canada by
Kids Can Press Ltd.
29 Birch Avenue
Toronto, ON M4V 1E2

Published in the U.S. by
Kids Can Press Ltd.
2250 Military Road
Tonawanda, NY 14150

www.kidscanpress.com

The artwork in this book was rendered in watercolor and marker.
The text is set in Smile.

Edited by Debbie Rogosin
Designed by Marie Bartholomew
Printed and bound in Hong Kong, China, by Book Art Inc., Toronto

The hardcover edition of this book is smyth sewn casebound.
The paperback edition of this book is limp sewn with a drawn-on cover.

CM 00 0 9 8 7 6 5 4 3 2 1
CM PA 02 0 9 8 7 6 5 4 3 2 1

National Library of Canada Cataloguing in Publication Data

Johansen, K. V. (Krista V.), 1968–
Pippin and the bones

(Pippin and Mabel)
ISBN 1-55074-629-4 (bound).   ISBN 1-55337-419-3 (pbk.)

I. Lum, Bernice II. Title. III. Series: Johansen, K. V. (Krista V.), 1968– . Pippin and Mabel.

PS8569.O2676P55 2000   jC813'.54   C99-932044-0
PZ7.J63Pi 2000

Kids Can Press is a Corus™ Entertainment company

Pippin and the Bones

Story by K.V. Johansen

Illustrations by Bernice Lum

Kids Can Press

Pippin was a yellow dog with great big ears and a curly black tail. She loved chewing on bones, and she loved digging holes. She buried her bones in the holes, to keep them safe from other dogs.

One day Mabel was digging in her garden. Pippin thought Mabel was looking for bones, so she began digging too.

"Thanks, but I don't need any help," said Mabel. She got a big beef bone and gave it to Pippin. "Here's a treat for you instead."

Pippin wagged her tail and ran behind the rosebushes to chew on her bone. Scrape! Scrunch! Crunch! Then she dug a hole and buried the bone.

"Oh no!" said Mabel when she saw the heap of mud. "What have you done to my lawn?" Mabel dug up Pippin's bone. She filled in the hole and jumped up and down on the lawn until it was flat again.

"Take your bone away," said Mabel, and she tossed it across the yard.

Pippin found her bone and bounded off to the garden to chew on it. Scrape! Scrunch! Crunch! Then she dug a hole and buried it. Now her bone would be safe!

"Oh no!" said Mabel when she saw the mountain of mud and roots. "What have you done to my tomatoes?"

Mabel dug up Pippin's bone and replanted her tomatoes.

"Take your bone away," said Mabel. "Far away!" She threw Pippin's bone right out of the yard.

Pippin grabbed her
bone and ran to the
woods. When she had gone
a long way, she lay down
to chew on her bone.
Scrape! Scrunch! Crunch!

Then she tried to dig a hole,
but the ground was too rocky. Pippin
ran farther into the woods and
tried to dig again, but
there were too many
tree roots.

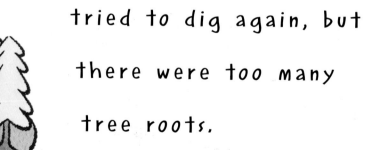

She ran a little farther and found a nice,
soft mossy spot, just right for burying a
bone. She began digging. This time
her bone would be safe,
even from Mabel.

Pippin dug
and dug. Then
she smelled
something good.
Mud flew through the
air as Pippin dug faster and faster.
She dug such a deep hole that not
even her tail stuck up over
the edge.

And she found ...

A huge old skull ...

great big tusks ...

and, best of all, bones!

Giant brown bones!

Pippin forgot about her beef bone and began
to chew on those giant brown bones. Scrape!
Scrunch! Crunch! So many bones, and they
were all hers!

Mabel finished her gardening. "Pippin!" she called. "Time for supper!"

But Pippin didn't come.

"Pippin!" Mabel called again. "Supper time!"

Still Pippin didn't come.

Mabel began to worry. Where was Pippin? What if she was hurt? Mabel ran to the woods. She found the rocky spot where Pippin had tried to dig, but she didn't find Pippin.

She saw the place where Pippin had dug in the tree roots, but she didn't see Pippin.

"Pippin!" she shouted. "Where are you?"

Pippin heard Mabel,
but she wouldn't leave
her bones. "Woof!" she said.
"Woof! Woof!"

Mabel followed
the sound until she
came to the hole.
She peered over the
edge at the skull and
the bones and the
enormous tusks.

"Oh my, Pippin!" said Mabel. "What have you found? That looks like an elephant, but elephants don't live in these woods!"

Mabel climbed into the hole and looked at the bones more closely. She'd never seen such huge bones.

"I don't think you should be chewing on these bones," Mabel said. "You'd better come home with me."

Mabel ran to the house, and Pippin galloped beside her. She hoped that Mabel was going to get the wheelbarrow so they could bring the bones home. Instead, Mabel phoned the museum.

The next day, some people from the museum came to see the bones.

"Incredible!" they said to Mabel. "Wonderful! Amazing! Your dog has found a mastodon skeleton!"

The museum people dug up the bones. Pippin started to dig too, but they didn't need any help. Then Pippin tried to hide a bone. The museum people found it.

The museum people put all the bones in a big truck and took them away. Now Pippin had no bones at all. Nothing was left except a big pile of mud. Pippin lay on top of it and moped.

Mabel gave Pippin a new ball to cheer her up. But it just wasn't the same.

One day a card for Pippin arrived in the mail.

"Look, Pippin," said Mabel.

"The museum has invited us to a mastodon party."

On the afternoon of the party there was a big crowd at the museum. Everyone admired the mastodon skeleton. Everyone wanted to pat Pippin and feed her ice cream and tell her what a clever dog she was. But Pippin looked at the bones and she sighed.

A photographer took a picture of Pippin with the mastodon and everybody clapped. Then the curator brought out a fancy box with a big red bow on top.

"This didn't belong to the mastodon," she said, setting the box in front of Pippin.

Mabel untied the bow.

Inside the box was ... Pippin's beef bone! Pippin wagged her tail. She forgot all about the mastodon.

She lay down right there on the museum floor to chew on her bone. Scrape! Scrunch! Crunch!

"Hmmm," said Mabel. "I have an idea. Maybe you can keep your bone safe in the box from now on, instead of in my garden!"

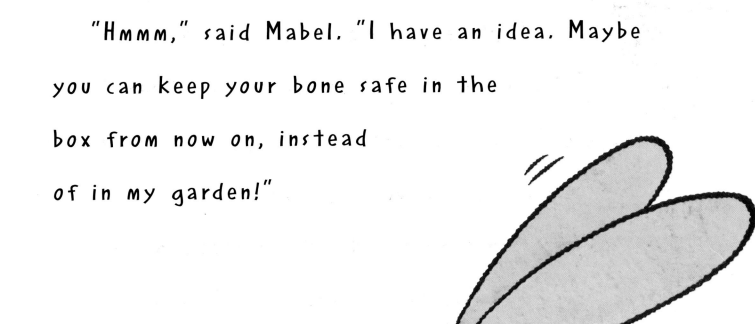

But Pippin had her own idea.

"Oh Pippin," said Mabel.

"Woof!" said Pippin.